# I
# WANT
# MY
# HAT
# BACK

For Will and Justin

ISBN 978-1-338-28355-6

12 11 10 9 8 7 6                                        21 22 23

Printed in the U.S.A.                                        76

First Scholastic printing, January 2018

This book was typeset in New Century Schoolbook.
The illustrations were created digitally and in Chinese ink.

# I
# WANT
# MY
# HAT
# BACK

## JON KLASSEN

SCHOLASTIC INC.

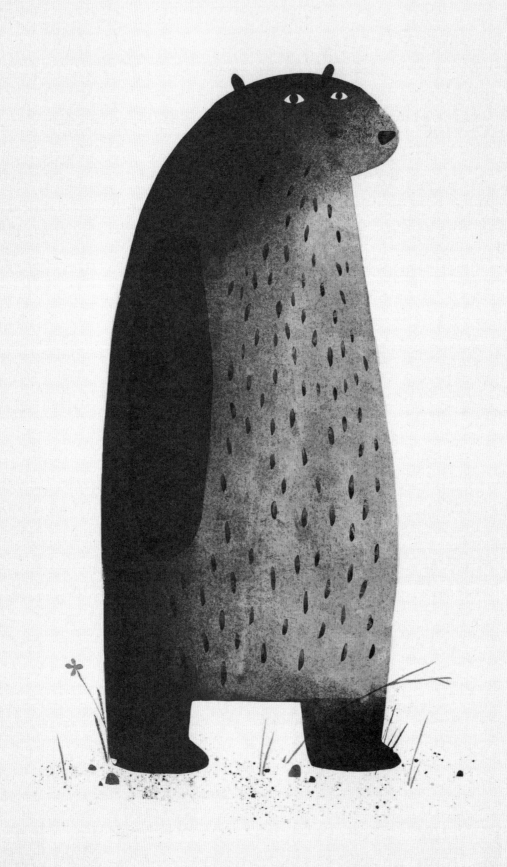

My hat is gone.
I want it back.

Have you seen my hat?

No. I haven't seen your hat.

OK. Thank you anyway.

Have you seen my hat?

No. I have not seen any hats around here.

OK. Thank you anyway.

Have you seen my hat?

No. Why are you asking me.
I haven't seen it.
I haven't seen any hats anywhere.
I would not steal a hat.
Don't ask me any more questions.

OK. Thank you anyway.

Have you seen my hat?

I haven't seen anything all day. I have been trying to climb this rock.

Would you like me to lift you on top of it?

Yes, please.

Have you seen my hat?

I saw a hat once.
It was blue and round.

My hat doesn't look like that.
Thank you anyway.

Have you seen my hat?

What is a hat?

Thank you anyway.

Nobody has seen my hat.
What if I never see it again?
What if nobody ever finds it?

My poor hat.
I miss it so much.

What's the matter?

I have lost my hat.
And nobody has seen it.

What does your hat look like?

It is red and pointy and . . .

# I HAVE
# SEEN MY HAT.

# YOU. YOU STOLE MY HAT.

I love my hat.

Excuse me, have you seen
a rabbit wearing a hat?

No. Why are you asking me.
I haven't seen him.
I haven't seen any rabbits
anywhere.
I would not eat a rabbit.
Don't ask me any more questions.

OK. Thank you anyway.

# JON KLASSEN

is the author-illustrator of

*This Is Not My Hat,* winner of the

Caldecott Medal and a *New York Times*

bestseller. He is also the illustrator of

*House Held Up by Trees* by Ted Kooser,

a *New York Times Book Review* Best

Illustrated Children's Book of the

Year, and *Extra Yarn* by Mac Barnett,

which was awarded a Caldecott Honor.

Originally from Niagara Falls, Ontario,

Jon Klassen now lives in California.